BAD LUCK
BOY

SUSANNAH BRIN

P.O. Box 355, Buena Park, CA 90621

Take Ten Books
Romance

Other Take Ten Themes:
Mystery
Sports
Adventure
Chillers
Thrillers
Disaster
Horror
Fantasy

Project Editor: Dwayne Epstein
Assistant Editor: Molly Mraz
Illustrations: Fujiko
Graphic Design: Tony Amaro
©2003 Artesian Press

www.artesianpress.com

 ISBN 1-58659-458-3

CONTENTS

Chapter 1

The morning fog just started to lift off the bay when Megan Thomas walked toward Ed's Diner. She searched the water for her father's lobster boat, the *Marylou*. Several boats were close to shore, but the *Marylou* wasn't one of them. *He's probably on the other side of Bailey's Island*, she thought.

When Megan entered the diner, she saw that it was nearly empty. The only people inside were the owner, Ed Stover, and someone washing dishes in the back. Megan wasn't surprised. It was almost ten A.M., and she knew that no self-respecting islander would ever be caught sitting in the diner in the middle of the morning.

"Morning, Megan. What have you got for me today?" asked Ed Stover. He looked up from the notes he was making on a piece of paper. Megan noticed Ed's white apron already had several coffee stains and one red splatter that she hoped was ketchup.

"Mom made two wild blueberry pies and two peach pies," Megan said. She put the pie baskets up onto the white tile counter.

"That sounds good. Tell her I could use some more brown bread and yeast rolls. Customers love her bread with my Boston baked beans. I guess the combination of the two foods is a winner," Ed said.

"I think she is baking you some bread right now, Ed. At least, it sure smelled like it when I left home," Megan said. She placed the pies on the counter. "Where's Mrs. Stover this morning?"

Ed made a new pot of coffee.

"She's over at the Inn. Sally Homer feels ill today, so Ruby is helping her make the beds and clean up the rooms. I reckon she'll be back in time for the lunch crowd. The diner's been getting busier with all the summer folks returning to the island," Ed answered.

"I know. I saw John Blackstone and his family yesterday. Dad says the Fishers are back, too," Megan said. She placed the blue-checked napkins that covered the pies back into the baskets.

Ed grinned. "You know the Blackstones' and the Fishers' grandparents came over on the same ship as my great-granddaddy. Back then, they made a living from the sea, just like the rest of us."

"I heard that the Blackstones made money during Prohibition by carrying illegal liquor in their boats," said Danny Doyle. He walked through the swinging door from the kitchen and into the front of the restaurant. He walked to the counter and bent down to pick up a plastic tub of dirty dishes. He looked up at Megan and smiled. "Hi, Megan," Danny said.

"Hi, Danny," said Megan. She looked at him and wondered why she'd never noticed how green his eyes were. They were dark green, like a stormy sea. When she realized that she was staring at him, she forced herself to look away. "I didn't know you worked here. I thought you worked at one of the fish stands down by the wharf."

"I'm filling in for my little brother. He had to go to the dentist this morning." Danny lifted the tub of dirty dishes like it was light as a feather.

"Danny is looking around for a job as a helper on the back of a lobster boat. He wants to be a sternman, isn't that right?" asked Ed.

"Yeah, but it seems all the lobster boats around here have already got a sternman or two," Danny said. His handsome face suddenly frowned as though he were angry. He stared at Megan, as if daring her to say the real reason no one would hire him.

Megan didn't look at Danny. Instead, she fussed with the lids on her baskets.

Like everyone else on the island, she knew why no one wanted to hire Danny Doyle. He and what was left of his family were considered bad luck. His father and two older brothers had died at sea. Some of the lobstermen said their deaths could have been prevented if luck had been on their side.

"Maybe you'll have to go down the coast to look for work," Ed said.

"I doubt I'd find anything," Danny said. "Word spreads."

Megan felt bad for him. She was not like most of the people on the island. She didn't believe that Danny was the "bad luck boy," as he was called when he wasn't around. She asked, "Why don't you ask my father? I heard him say the other day he was looking for a new helper."

Danny stopped on his way to the kitchen and turned back toward Megan. "I thought Jamie Davis was your dad's sternman," he said.

"His arthritis is so bad, he can barely pull the lines," Megan said.

Danny's face looked hopeful. He grinned. "I'll talk to your father then. Thanks, Megan."

Megan smiled. "Okay, well see you, Danny, Ed," she said. She hoped they didn't suspect how nervous she was feeling all of a sudden. *Why did I open my big mouth?* she thought.

Megan hurried down the street toward her house. She could already hear her father yelling at her. She had no right to offer a job on his boat. Offering one to the "bad luck boy" only made things worse.

Chapter 2

It had already started to get dark when Patrick Thomas came through the back door. He worked a twelve-hour day. His weathered face looked tired.

Patrick lowered himself into a chair at the kitchen table. He waited while his wife, Mary, brought him a mug of hot coffee. "Where's Megan?" he asked.

"In her room. Why?" asked Mary. She wiped her hands on her faded green apron.

Patrick shook his head slowly and smiled like he was amused. "That girl of ours is at it again."

"What has she gone and done now?" asked Mary. She knew that

their daughter Megan often found stray animals—and sometimes people—and offered them all some sort of help. They already had two orphaned dogs and a one-eyed cat that Megan rescued.

"She went and found me a replacement for Jamie Davis," said Patrick. As he was about to say more, Megan walked into the kitchen.

"Oh, did you hire Danny Doyle?" Megan asked. She had heard some of the conversation.

"Danny Doyle? From that bad luck Doyle family?" asked Mary with surprise.

"The same," said Patrick. He drank some of his coffee and looked at his wife and daughter.

"Mom, I wish you wouldn't call his family bad luck," Megan said.

"Would you rather I called them stubborn?" Mary asked. She turned to the stove and lifted the lid on a large pot of stew. She stirred the stew as she kept talking. "Everyone told them not to paint their boat blue, but they didn't listen," she said. "First, the father is killed in an accident at sea, then the two brothers. Everyone knows you don't fish in a blue boat. Blue boats are bad luck. Everyone says bad luck has found a home with the Doyle family," she said.

"You don't believe that, do you, Dad?" Megan asked. She looked at her father's face to see how he really felt.

"Danny seems like a good kid. I want to give him a try as my sternman for the summer," said Patrick. His brown eyes twinkled. "I'm not a superstitious person like your mother. But to be on the safe side, you'd never catch me painting my lobster boat blue."

Megan laughed. She wrapped her arms around her father's neck and gave him a hug. Then she slipped into her chair as her mother brought the steaming pot of stew to the table.

After a dinner of salad, stew, and cornbread, Mary served fresh blueberry pie. Megan asked for ice cream on hers, as did her father. "It's a good thing we're all thin in this family, the way we eat," Mary said. She laughed and topped her pie with a big scoop of ice cream, too.

Megan made a face. "I don't know what's so great about being thin. I almost look like a boy."

Her father reached out and messed up Megan's short blond hair. "You look fine to me and to Danny Doyle too, I bet."

Megan pushed her father's hand away, annoyed. "Danny just goes to my school, okay? I ran into him at Ed's Diner and he said he was looking for a job."

"He's a good-looking young man," Patrick said. Megan saw him wink at her mom.

"Dad, will you stop it, please? He's not even a close friend," Megan said. She got up from the table. She could feel that her cheeks were hot from embarrassment.

She was telling the truth. She hardly knew Danny. It was only today——when he'd looked at her with those dark green eyes of his———that she'd really seen him. He'd made her heart beat faster and her stomach feel jumpy.

Megan put her dirty dishes in the sink and walked to the back door. "I'll do the dishes later, Mom."

"No, you've done a lot of running down to the diner for me today. I'll do them," said Mary.

"Megan, why don't you come out on the boat tomorrow? You can band the lobster claws while I show Danny how to haul the traps," Patrick said.

"All right," Megan said. She went out the back door and took a deep breath. The air was damp and smelled like the sea. Stars twinkled in the sky and a full moon shone brightly on the bay. Megan walked toward the harbor. It was June, but the nights were still chilly.

As she passed Ed's Diner, John Blackstone and Chelsea Fisher came out of the doorway. They were laughing and talking with a couple of other kids Megan didn't know. Megan tried to get away without being seen, but John Blackstone saw her.

"Megan Thomas, is that you?" John asked. He grabbed her arm and spun her toward him so he could see her face better.

"Hi, John. I heard you were back," Megan said with a smile. *John isn't so bad,* she thought to herself. She just didn't want to spend her summer listening to him brag about himself. John liked to talk about how good he was at just about everything.

When they were little, they were close friends. They built sand castles on the beach together, but that was years ago.

"I sure hope you weren't going to just walk on by without saying hello," John said.

"No, I just didn't see you there," Megan lied. She turned toward Chelsea Fisher. "Hi, Chelsea. I heard you were back, too."

"Yes. I wanted to go to Europe, but Daddy just loves it out here on the island during the summer. He said we'd go to Paris for Christmas," Chelsea said. She sounded bored and a little irritated.

You need to be less of a snob, Megan wanted to tell Chelsea. Instead she made herself smile. "I can't imagine Christmas any place but here on the island," Megan said.

"We're all going down to the yacht club to hang out. Why don't you come with us?" John asked.

"Thanks, but I'm just out for a walk. I've got to get back and help Mom with the dishes," Megan lied again.

She didn't want to go with them to the club. She knew some club members frowned on locals being at the club unless they worked there.

"Well, come by the yacht harbor tomorrow. I'm going to get my boat out of dry dock. I'll take you for a sail," John said. He and the others walked off and Chelsea waved.

Megan watched the group turn the corner and disappear into the night. She realized she should have told John that she wouldn't be able to stop by. She would be on her father's lobster boat instead.

She thought about Danny Doyle and smiled. Megan looked up at the stars and wondered if this was the summer she would fall in love.

Megan looked up at the stars and wondered if this was the summer she would fall in love.

Chapter 3

It was still dark as Megan and her father walked to the boat. Megan shivered in the cold air and wished she was back in her warm bed. "Why do you start the day so early, Dad? The sun isn't even up yet."

"In the morning, a land breeze usually blows out over the ocean. By midday, that same breeze can get strong and stir up large waves. Big waves bounce everything and make it hard to work on the boat," Patrick said.

Megan yawned. "That makes sense, but the bouncing has to be better than getting up so early."

Patrick chuckled. "You've never been out on rough seas or you wouldn't say that, darling."

The harbor was busy with all kinds of activity. Megan could hear boat motors start, sea gulls squawk, men yell, and water hit the sides of the dock. All these sounds meant that another day was starting for the lobstermen. Megan's father greeted everyone, but he didn't stop to chat.

As Megan reached the dock where her father kept his fishing boat, she saw Danny Doyle. He waited next to the boat. Four fish baskets full of herring, a kind of fish, sat on the dock by his feet. Megan guessed her father had told him to bring the boxes of herring to use for bait.

"Morning, Danny," said Patrick. He looked at Danny as he spoke.

"Morning, sir," Danny said. He smiled at Megan and she felt her heart beat faster. "I got the bait you wanted."

"Good," said Patrick, as he stepped

onto the boat. "I hope you brought some oversized boots with you."

Danny followed Patrick onto the boat. "No, sir." He looked down at his tennis shoes.

"Well, have Megan find you a pair down below. On my boat, we wear oversized boots and oversized gloves. If you get a foot or a hand tangled in a line as it goes out, there's a good chance you'll end up in the water. The heavy gear could drag you to the bottom. So you see, I'd rather have a boot or glove go into the water. Didn't your father ever teach you that?"

Danny shrugged. "My father wasn't much of a teacher, Mr. Thomas."

Patrick grunted and turned on the boat's engine. Megan went down into the galley, the boat's kitchen, to put the lunch in the fridge. She found two extra pairs of boots and gloves. She pulled on a pair of boots. She handed the other pair to Danny, who had followed her down to the galley.

"Thanks, and thanks for getting me this job," Danny said. He smiled at Megan.

The room was so small that Megan couldn't help but notice everything about him. When she realized he was staring at her, too, she turned her head shyly. "My father gave you the job, not me."

"Well, you told me about it. So thanks, I owe you one," Danny said. He turned and went back up on deck.

Patrick steered the thirty-six-foot-long boat through the harbor and out into Casco Bay. It was five-thirty, and the sun was rising.

Megan grabbed her gloves, pulled her knitted cap down around her ears, and climbed up on deck. Danny stood next to Patrick and listened to instructions. Megan swayed as the boat surged through the water. It left behind a wake of foamy white waves.

"Once we get out of the bay and on the other side of Bailey's Island, we'll find my markers, or *buoys*. Mine are orange and green," said Patrick.

"How many traps do you have out?" Danny asked.

"I have eight hundred traps in the water. We fish one-third of the traps each day until we've gotten through them all. Then we start over. Each group of traps stays on the bottom for three days, which gives us a better chance to catch lobsters. After I haul the traps in, you will empty them and then bait them. Then we can drop them back in," Patrick said.

Megan watched Danny. She wondered why she'd never noticed what a good-looking boy he was with his stormy green eyes and curly brown hair. She was 5'5" tall and he was only a few inches taller. She guessed he was about 5'11". *Just the right height for me*, Megan thought.

At that moment, Danny turned and caught her staring at him. Megan almost choked. She was afraid he knew what she was thinking.

When they reached the first buoy, Patrick stopped the boat. He grabbed a big hook to bring in the buoy. Once he had the buoy in the hook, he started the hauler. The hauler brought the traps up and laid them on the rail. Patrick showed Danny how to clean out the lobster traps.

"All female lobsters with eggs have to be returned to the sea," Patrick said. We also put back any lobsters under five inches long. Legal-size lobsters are called *keepers*. We put the keepers in a tank. We throw the small lobsters, or *shorts* as we like to call them, back in the water so they can grow bigger."

Sea gulls hung in the sky near the side of the boat. They swooped down to grab old bait as Danny threw it in the water. The gulls squawked and acted like fighting children. After she pulled on her gloves, Megan took the lobsters from the box and measured them.

"Be really careful with the females, Megan. We want those eggs to hatch into more lobsters," Patrick said. Megan handed him an egg-bearing lobster and he gently put it back in the sea.

After Megan decided that a lobster was a keeper, she put bands around its strong, sharp claws. Then she put the lobster into a tank of fresh seawater.

Danny cleaned out the traps. He worked with speed and total concentration. His job was to clean the traps and fill the bait pouches. He was done after just a short time. "I'm all ready for you to reset the trap lines," Danny said.

Megan noticed her father seemed to be happy with the work Danny had done. Megan was glad. Her father began to reset the traps in the water along with their buoys. Danny squatted next to the boxes of lobsters and helped her band the lobster claws. "That went pretty fast, don't you think?" Danny asked. He leaned close to Megan so he would not have to yell.

Megan grinned. "That was just the first set of traps. We'll be doing this all day."

When the traps were down on the sea floor again, Patrick started the boat. They sailed across the water toward the next buoy to begin the routine again.

While they were on the way to the next set of buoys, Megan and Danny rested. Megan thought Danny was easy to talk to. She wondered why she'd never gotten to know him before. She thought they liked a lot of the same things.

As it got later in the day, the work got harder. By late afternoon, Megan and Danny slowed down. Patrick must have noticed they were tired. As he drank his cup of coffee, he reminded them that the day wasn't over. They still had to sell the lobsters to the dealer on shore and clean up the boat.

After the last trap was emptied and reset, the boat headed for home. Danny stretched and sat down next to Megan. "Whoa, I haven't worked this hard in a long time," Danny said. He rolled his shoulders to loosen his neck muscles. "Are you going to keep working on the boat?"

Megan nodded. She thought to herself that there was nothing she would like better than to spend the summer working next to Danny. Now all she had to do was to convince her father he needed her help, too.

Chapter 4

When Megan asked her father if she could work on the boat, too, he said yes. He was pleased. Megan went out lobstering with her father and Danny all week.

The work was hard, but she liked being on the boat. She especially liked to spend time with Danny, getting to know him.

Everything was going fine until Saturday. The day started out okay, but then it began to rain. The rain fell hard as they hauled in the first set of traps. They worked quickly. When they were done, they went into the boat's wheelhouse to dry off.

They reached a spot where another

set of buoys were dropped earlier. They expected to find the buoys, but they didn't see anything. Patrick turned the boat's motor to idle and climbed on top of the wheelhouse roof for a better look. There were no buoys in sight. He jumped down, went back inside the wheelhouse, and started the boat.

There was nothing they could do, so they sailed toward the next set of buoys. Megan asked, "Where do you think those buoys went?"

"They probably got taken out by a big fishing boat like a trawler or a barge. It happens. Hopefully, the gear will wash up on one of the beaches. It's bad luck, but it happens," said Patrick.

Danny stepped out of the wheelhouse. He stood alone out on the deck in the pouring rain.

Patrick frowned and gave Megan a questioning look. "You said *bad luck*,

Dad. He probably thinks that *you* think the buoys are gone because he has 'bad luck,'" Megan said.

"It's no one's fault. If Danny thought that I meant *he* was bad luck, then he's a little too sensitive. I meant no such thing," Patrick said. He looked serious.

Megan joined Danny on deck. She snapped the buttons closed on her slicker jacket and pulled the drawstring on the hood to keep out the rain. "What's wrong?"

Danny kept staring at the ocean. He looked like he was searching for the lost buoys.

"Come back inside. The wind is really starting to blow out here," Megan said. The rain stung her face like tiny insect bites.

"I'm fine," Danny said.

"My dad didn't mean anything when he said it was bad luck losing the gear," Megan said.

"I know that. It's just sometimes I begin to believe all that stuff about me being a 'bad luck boy' from a bad luck family," Danny said.

"I believe you make your own luck," Megan said stubbornly.

Danny looked at Megan. "Well, it was lucky for me that I ran into you at Ed's Diner. Just think, we could have spent the rest of our lives never getting to know each other." He smiled a little and his body relaxed. His green eyes looked first at her eyes, then at her lips, and then at her eyes again.

Megan looked at Danny's mouth. She felt like she wanted to be closer to him. *He's going to kiss me*, she thought, feeling very excited.

Just then, the boat stopped. Megan looked past Danny at the ocean. Orange-and-green buoys bobbed in the water. It was time to get back to work.

Chapter 5

By late afternoon, all the traps had been emptied and rebaited. Patrick turned the boat for home. The ocean was choppy from the rain and the wind. The boat plowed through the large waves, sending a spray of water across the bow.

From the wheelhouse, Megan could see her father. He stared straight ahead, his mouth shut tightly. Megan knew he was upset.

First, there were the missing lobster traps and buoys; second, the other traps had been almost empty. Instead of getting seven hundred to a thousand lobsters, they had gotten fewer than a hundred for the whole day.

"Maybe it's the rain, Dad. Maybe the lobsters don't like to come out from under their rocks when it's raining," Megan said. She wanted to cheer him up.

Patrick shook his head. "I don't know what is keeping the lobsters away from the traps. This has never happened in all my years of lobstering."

"Maybe that part of the ocean floor is fished out," said Danny. "We should move the traps and gear to another spot further out."

"And just where would that be exactly?" Patrick asked. He gave Danny a serious look.

Danny didn't give up. "I heard no one has fished close in to Round Rock Island for years."

"It's too dangerous to fish there. Beneath the sandbanks, there are underwater ledges that can rip the hull of a boat quicker than you can say *halibut*," Patrick said. He slowed the boat as it neared the harbor.

"Well, I heard my father and brothers talk about all the lobsters out there just waiting to be caught," Danny said.

"Your family never thought about the danger of anything, and look what happened to them. Three deadly accidents that could have been avoided, son," Patrick said. "And that is why everyone around here says your family has bad luck. It wasn't bad luck—it was foolish thinking," Patrick added.

Megan saw Danny's face turn red when her father talked about his father and brothers. She knew an argument was coming, and she tried to stop it. "Dad, I think Danny is just trying to be helpful."

"I don't need help lobstering. I've been doing it since before either of you were born," Patrick said. He guided the boat into its place at the dock and turned off the motor.

Danny ran out of the wheelhouse. He jumped up on the dock and began to moor the boat, or tie the lines from the boat to the dock.

"Dad, how could you say all those things to Danny?" Megan asked.

Patrick turned from the wheel and looked at her. "The truth will help him. I only spoke the truth as I see it."

"What if he quits?" Megan asked. She hated the idea.

"Why would he do that?" Patrick asked. "If your friend has any guts, he'll keep working for me and know I meant him no harm."

Megan shook her head and went out on deck. The rain had turned to a light mist. She could see Danny dragging the dockside hose over to the boat. She wanted to talk to him but she didn't know what to say. She just hoped he wouldn't quit.

Chapter 6

On Sunday, they didn't fish for lobster. In Maine, it is illegal to haul traps on Sundays from June 1 to September 1.

Megan was glad. She was tired, so she slept late. When she finally got up, she noticed the rain had stopped. It was a beautiful day, without a cloud in the bright blue sky.

After a quick breakfast of her mother's homemade granola and milk, Megan lifted the pie baskets off the kitchen counter. She left for Ed's Diner. Her father might not go lobstering, but her mother baked for the diner every day.

On her way to Ed's Diner, Megan

saw Chelsea Fisher. Chelsea was talking and waving her hands as a young man squatted down by the front wheel of her bike. Megan groaned. She did not look forward to having a conversation with Chelsea, but there wasn't any way to get away from her.

As Megan got closer, Chelsea saw her. "Megan, can you believe it? My bike had a flat tire! I don't know why it has a flat. I haven't ridden my bike since last summer," Chelsea squealed.

"Maybe it has a slow leak and just needs some air, Chelsea," Megan said. The young man whose back was to Megan turned and looked at her. Megan blinked. It was Danny.

"Hey, Megan," Danny said. He gave her a big smile as he stood up.

"Danny saved me. My bike went out of control and I was about to fall just as he was walking by. He just reached out and steadied the bike. Now he's going with me to the gas station to help me get the tire fixed," Chelsea said. She smiled at Danny like he was her hero.

Megan thought Chelsea was just about the dumbest girl she'd ever met. Then she saw that Danny was looking at Chelsea, and Megan thought again. Maybe Chelsea wasn't as dumb as Megan thought. After all, she'd just met Danny and already he was doing whatever she wanted.

Megan wanted to stomp her foot in anger, but instead she kept smiling. "Danny is very helpful. I'll bet once your tire is fixed, he'll even ride around the island with you and show you the sights," Megan said. Her smile became stiffer by the minute.

Chelsea smiled at Danny. "What a great idea! Doesn't that sound like fun, Danny?"

Danny didn't answer. He just grinned like he was enjoying himself.

"I've got to deliver these pies,"

Megan said. She didn't look at Danny.

"See ya," Chelsea said.

Megan took a deep breath and started walking. When she reached Ed's Diner, she went inside. Through the window she saw Danny pushing Chelsea's bike as Chelsea walked next to him.

"Morning, Megan. Bringing the pies, are you?" asked Ed.

"Yes," Megan sighed. She placed the two baskets on the counter. "Peach and strawberry. Two of each kind."

"What's the matter? You look pretty angry," Ed said. He placed the pies in a refrigerated cupboard on the wall behind the counter.

"Oh, nothing really. See ya," Megan said. She picked up the empty baskets and headed for the door. *I am so stupid*, Megan thought to herself. *Danny Doyle isn't interested in me. He's just being nice because I got him a job.* She remembered how she thought he was going to kiss her on the boat. "Yeah, right," she said aloud.

"Who are you talking to?" asked a male voice.

Megan looked up and saw John Blackstone stepping off the sidewalk toward her. "Just talking to myself."

"It's okay to talk to yourself as long as you don't answer yourself, too. If you start answering yourself then we'll all know you're crazy," John said. He gave her a big smile.

Megan made a face at him for teasing her. "I'll remember that."

"I was just heading down to the yacht club to go sailing. Want to come along?" John asked.

Megan was going to say no, but then she thought about Danny and Chelsea. She imagined them together, riding bikes, talking, and laughing. "Sure. Sounds like fun."

Chapter 7

Once they left the harbor and rounded Bailey's Island, Megan began to relax and enjoy herself. A brisk breeze whipped the water into whitecaps and sent the sailboat gliding quickly through the water. "I forgot how much fun sailing is. It's so different from Dad's boat with its diesel engine."

"Well, a sailboat isn't meant for fishing," John said. "It's meant for racing or for just enjoying the ride through the water."

"I never thought about it like that, John, but you're right. There is something romantic about a sailboat." Megan turned her face into the wind, letting it ruffle her hair.

"Let's go sailing at night sometime, if you want romantic," John said with a wink.

Megan shook her head and laughed. "Don't get any ideas, John. I was talking about sailing like a poet would talk when I said it was romantic," she said.

"Yeah, well, I'm serious about us sailing at night. We could tie up on one of the deserted islands and have a big clambake or something like that."

"Let's have a clambake closer to home," Megan said. She didn't want to sail anywhere with John at night. She especially wouldn't go near any of the small islands where hidden rocky ledges might rip a hole in the bottom of a boat.

"Take the wheel for a moment, Megan," John said. He stood up and began to untie the front sail, called the *spinnaker*. The spinnaker was a large triangular sail with red and blue stripes. It swung out opposite the mainsail. "Don't tell me you believe the stories about those islands being haunted."

"No, but I do think the rocky ledges around some of these islands are very dangerous in low tides. Even the best fishermen stay away from them."

John laughed. "You don't have to tell me. I learned to sail in these waters. I know this area as well as I know my own face."

As the sailboat picked up speed, Megan stopped talking. She enjoyed the feeling of speeding across the water with the wind and ocean spray in her face.

After a couple of hours, they lowered the sails and used the motor to cruise into the yacht club harbor where John guided his boat to the dock. Megan jumped out of the boat and helped him tie it to the dock.

"I'm starving. How about you?"

John asked.

"I could eat something," Megan said. They headed up the ramp toward the landing. As they turned toward the yacht club, Megan saw Danny standing by his car in the club's parking lot. *What is he doing here?* she wondered.

Then she saw Danny's sister Katie. Apparently, Katie had gotten a job as a waitress at the club and was just now getting off work. It wasn't unusual for local girls to work at the club during the summer.

"Isn't that Danny Doyle and his sister over there?" John asked. He raised his hand to wave at them.

Megan wished she was invisible. Danny saw her and stared. He didn't wave or smile. He just got in his car and slammed the door.

Who does he think he is? Megan thought. All she could think about was how he had helped Chelsea with her bike earlier in the day.

Chapter 8

The next week, Megan and Danny worked side by side on the lobster boat. They were polite, but they hardly spoke to each other. Their unspoken suspicions separated them like a cement wall. By Friday afternoon, Patrick was tired of the stony silence on the boat.

"What is going on between you and Danny?" Patrick asked. He looked at Megan as they stood together in the small wheelhouse. The boat was headed toward the next set of buoys.

"Nothing," Megan answered. She could see Danny outside on the deck. He leaned against the metal railing.

"Don't give me that. Things are pretty tense on this boat. I thought you liked him," Patrick said.

Megan didn't want to admit, even to her father, that her feelings had been hurt. "I don't know where you got that idea. He likes Chelsea Fisher, one of the summer people." At least she thought he did, when she remembered how he helped Chelsea with her bike.

Patrick raised an eyebrow as he looked at his daughter. "Oh, so that's it. You're jealous."

Losing her temper, Megan said, "I'm not jealous!"

"What about John Blackstone? Do you like him?" asked Patrick. He looked out at the open sea, searching for his orange-and-green buoys.

"We're just friends. We've been friends forever," Megan said. She knew that her father already knew how she felt about John.

"Does Danny know that?" Patrick asked as he stopped the boat.

"What is this, Twenty Questions?"

The next week, Megan and Danny worked side by side on the lobster boat. They were polite, but they hardly spoke to each other.

Megan asked. Not waiting for an answer, she left the wheelhouse as the boat pulled up to another set of buoys.

The hauler lifted the traps out of the water. Danny took lobsters from the trap and Megan banded the claws. Looking up from her job, Megan saw John's sailboat headed straight for them. Her father saw it, too.

"What is that fool doing?" Patrick asked. He watched as John zigzagged the sailboat through the water.

"It doesn't look like he can hold a steady course," Danny said. He looked at Megan. "Or maybe he's coming over to ask Megan to go sailing again."

"I don't care what he's doing. I don't want him getting too close to my boat and my gear. I don't need an accident," Patrick said.

John sailed his boat almost up to the lobster boat. At the last minute, he turned to the right, just missing the bow. In fact, they came so close,

Megan could plainly see John and Chelsea.

John called out a hello and Chelsea stood up and waved. *I hope she falls in*, Megan thought. She saw that Chelsea seemed to be looking just at Danny.

"Your boyfriend sure is an idiot to sail so close to us," Danny said.

"He's not my boyfriend. Besides, your girlfriend isn't all that smart, either," said Megan. She put a band around a lobster claw with a loud snap.

Danny stopped baiting the lobster trap in front of him. He turned and gave Megan a quizzical look. He opened his mouth to say something, but then he just shook his head and went back to work.

By the time they finished pulling and resetting all the lobster traps, it was late afternoon. The fog was so thick, they couldn't see anything. The slap of the ocean waves against the boat and the lonely wail of the foghorn filled the silence.

Patrick was about to head for home when they heard the ship-to-shore radio. "Mayday, mayday, mayday! This is John Blackstone on the vessel *Wind Surfer*, I.D. number, Larry-Tango-Gulf 343. We've hit a reef. Mayday, mayday, mayday!"

"Oh my gosh, it's John," Megan said. She reached for the radio's microphone, but her father was faster.

"This is Patrick Thomas on the *Marylou*. Where are you, John?"

"Round Rock Island, I think!" yelled John. His voice was drowned out by the sound of wood breaking and a girl's screams. The radio squawked with static before it went silent.

Patrick grabbed the wheel and pushed the throttle to full speed ahead. The lobster boat almost jumped out of the water as it surged forward.

"Danny, get out the life preserver rings and place them on either side of the boat. Megan, you watch the radar screen for me. Let me know when you see the rocky ledges begin to rise off the ocean floor," said Patrick.

Megan nodded and looked down at the green screen. It showed the ocean floor as different colored lines and masses. It was like reading a map. On the radio they heard the voices of coast guard officers and lobstermen who also heard the mayday signal. Everyone was racing toward the ledges at Round Rock Island.

"Do you think John's boat has sunk?" Megan asked fearfully.

"Let's hope not. It's going to be hard enough to find the boat in this fog without having to search for people in the water," Patrick said.

"Dad, the ocean floor has just risen several thousand feet," Megan said as she read the radar screen. Patrick immediately slowed the engine to a crawl. He studied the lines on the screen that showed where the rocky ledges stuck out into the water from the island's edge.

Out on deck, Danny started yelling. "Stop the boat, I see something!"

Megan looked, too. She saw nothing, but then she heard John's voice. "Over here! We're over here!"

Patrick put the throttle into idle. The engines whined and the boat trembled as it stopped in the water. "We can't go any further in. It's low tide. The rocks will rip our hull to shreds as they did to John's boat," Patrick said.

"What are we going to do?" Megan asked. Her question was answered when she looked out on deck and saw Danny. He was busy lowering the boat's skiff into the water. In seconds, he was over the side, paddling the small boat toward the sound of the voices.

Chapter 9

The fog swirled around Megan as she stared into the grayish mass. She looked for Danny and the others. "I can't see anything. Can you?" she asked her father.

"No," said Patrick. He leaned over the railing to try to get a better view.

Suddenly, Megan could hear Danny's voice calling out instructions. "Over here!" he shouted. "Give her a hand into the boat." Then for a moment, the fog parted. Megan got a glimpse of Danny in the small boat.

"Danny's got them!" cried Patrick. He rushed to throw a rope ladder over the side. When Danny got the small boat up alongside the *Marylou*, he grabbed hold of the rope ladder and held it steady for Chelsea to climb.

When Chelsea reached the railing, Megan helped her up. Chelsea clung to Megan like she would never let go. "Hey, we'd better get you into some dry clothes," Megan said. She felt Chelsea shake with cold. She asked her father to help the boys and led Chelsea down below.

By the time Megan got Chelsea changed into warm, dry clothes, Patrick had pulled John and Danny back onto the boat. Megan carried blankets up on deck and handed them to John.

Patrick went back into the wheelhouse. He moved the lobster boat away from the dangerous rocks and out onto open waters. The fog rolled thickly across the choppy water and made it impossible to see more than a few feet ahead.

Patrick wasn't worried. He'd been in rougher weather and rougher seas.

The *Marylou* also carried very modern mapping equipment.

As the boat sped for home, Megan poured hot coffee for everyone. She handed a cup to John, who sat on deck wrapped in a blanket.

She could tell John was deeply frightened by the accident. He didn't talk. He only stared out at the fog. When he finally decided to say something, it was to Danny.

"Thanks, man. You saved our lives," said John sincerely. Chelsea came up on deck and she thanked Danny, too.

Danny shrugged like it was no big deal.

"Well, luck sure wasn't with me today," John said. He shook his head. "I can't believe I laid my sailboat up on the rocks."

"Luck doesn't have anything to do with what happened today," said Danny angrily. "It was stupid to sail so close to Round Rock Island, especially in a low tide and fog." Danny turned and went into the galley below.

"What's wrong with him?" John asked Megan.

"He's doesn't like the word *luck*. People in town call him the 'bad luck boy' because his father and brothers died in boating accidents," Megan said.

"That's awful," Chelsea said. "He saved our lives. He's a hero, not a 'bad luck boy.' I'm going to tell him so."

You just do that, Megan thought. She watched Chelsea get up and go down into the galley to talk to Danny.

"Hey, you look like an angry hornet all of a sudden," John said.

"I'm not. Let's go into the wheel-house. It's warmer in there. The cold is starting to affect your brain," Megan said. She tried not to look down into the galley to see what Danny and Chelsea were doing.

*Megan tried not to look down into the galley
to see what Danny and Chelsea were doing.*

"I radioed the coast guard and told them we've picked you up. I'm afraid your boat will be driftwood by tomorrow, if it's not sunk already," said Patrick. He steered the *Marylou* into the harbor.

John frowned. "I can't believe I was so stupid. I should have sailed for home when the fog began to gather."

Patrick nodded. "You can't ever stop thinking when you're on the ocean. Even the smallest mistake can lead to a disaster."

"I'm sure glad you were close by," John said. "And Danny. I don't think we could have stayed in that cold water much longer. You all saved our lives."

Megan smiled and thought about how brave Danny had been. He'd gone into the fog in the small boat without a thought for his own safety.

Later, after John and Chelsea left, Megan and Danny helped her father clean up the boat. "I'm going to take the lobster up to the dealer. See you tomorrow, Danny. Good job saving those kids today," said Patrick.

Megan pulled the wheelhouse door shut and snapped the lock. Then she walked across the deck to the rail. When her feet hit the wooden planks of the dock, she felt Danny's hand on her arm, steadying her.

"Thanks," Megan said. His touch sent a feeling like electricity up her arm. She pulled her arm loose as she stepped away from him. "You'd better get going if you want to catch up with Chelsea."

Danny smiled. "Don't you ever stop? I think Chelsea and John can find their own way home." Before Megan could answer, he leaned forward and kissed her gently on the lips.

Fog curled around them like a cloak. Out in the bay, a foghorn sounded a warning to passing ships.